The Selfish Crocodile
Book of
Nursery Rhymes

Faustin Charles

Illustrated by
Michael Terry

BLOOMSBURY
CHILDREN'S
BOOKS

Rock-a-bye birdie on the treetop,
When the wind blows the nest will rock;

First published in Great Britain in 2008 by Bloomsbury Publishing Plc
36 Soho Square, London, W1D 3QY

Text copyright © Faustin Charles 2008
Illustrations copyright © Michael Terry 2008
The moral rights of the author and illustrator have been asserted

Audio copyright in recording © and ℗ Bloomsbury Publishing Plc 2008
Music composed by Andy Quin and licensed by MPCS on behalf of De Wolfe Music

A CIP catalogue record of this book is available from the British Library

ISBN 978 0 7475 9523 6

Printed in China

1 3 5 7 9 10 8 6 4 2

www.bloomsbury.com/childrens

Mixed Sources
Product group from well-managed
forests, controlled sources and
recycled wood or fibre
www.fsc.org Cert no. SCS-COC-00927
© 1996 Forest Stewardship Council
FSC

When the branch breaks the nest will fall,
And down will come birdie, nest and all.

Little bird blue, come sing your song,
The chicks in the nest aren't very strong.
Where is the mummy who looks after their keep?
She's under the tree there, fast asleep!

One, two, three, four, five,

Once I caught a snake alive;

Six, seven, eight, nine, ten,

Then I let it go again.

Why did you let it go?

Because it bit my little toe.

Which toe did it bite?

This little red one on the right.

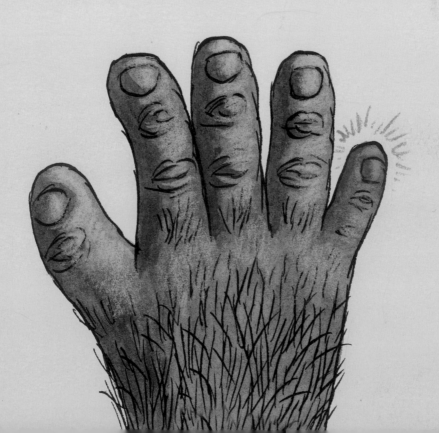

Three brave mice, three brave mice,
See how they run, see how they run;
They all ran after the crocodile,
Who gave them a hug and a toothy smile;
Did you ever see mice with such great style
As these three brave mice?

Little Zack Zebra

Stood by the river,

Eating the grass nearby.

He put out his tongue,

Then spat out a plum,

And said,
"What a good zebra am I!"

The racing wild deer ran down to the river
In a shower of rain.
He slipped on a stone, almost breaking a bone,
And never went down there again.

Zippy, Zippy, the greedy zebra,
Had a calf and couldn't keep her;
She put her in a tortoise shell
And there she kept her very well.

Chicks and cubs, come out to play,

The sun is shining every day;
Leave the nests and leave the pride,
And join us by the riverside.

Come with a swoop, come with a call,
Come with a cheer or not at all;
From the trees and from the ground,
We are waiting to hear the sound.

There was
an old lion
Who lived under a hill,
And if he's not gone,
He lives there still.

Teeth, teeth, shining bright,

Even in the darkest night.

Teeth, teeth, sharp and strong,

Teeth, teeth, white and long.

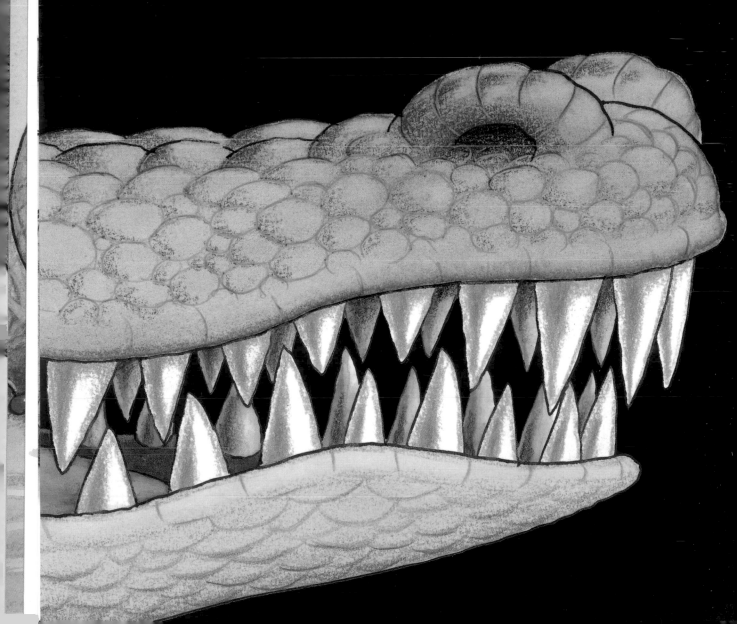

Little alligator
Yelled for his supper.

What shall he eat?
Berries and banana.
What shall he drink?
Warm river water.

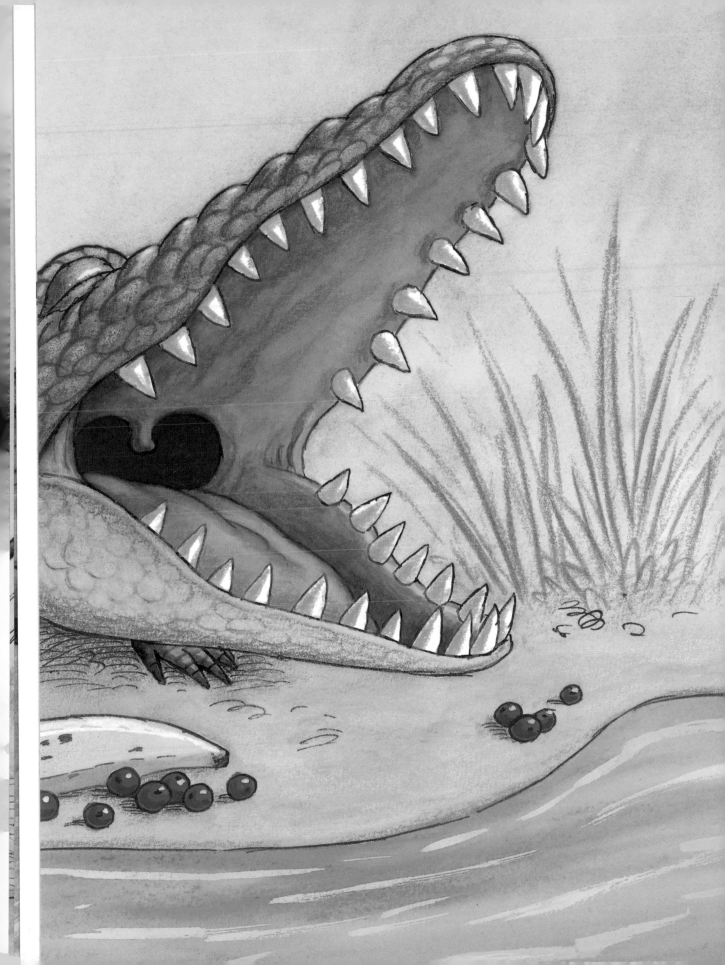